The Possible

Poems by
Bruce Bond

Winner of the 1993 Gerald Cable
Poetry Chapbook Competition
Silverfish Review Press

Poems from this chapbook first appeared in the following journals:

The Missouri Review	"Acoustic Shadows"
Poetry	"Prelude" (appeared as "On Certainty")
	"Taps"
Quarterly West	"New York Movie, 1939"
Sewanee Review	"The Confederate Dead"
	"Photograph of the 5th Vermont at Camp Griffin, Virginia"
Shenandoah	"The Possible"
Western Humanities Review	"Radiography"

"Taps," "The Possible," and "Prelude" (published as "On Certainty") were selected for the *Quarterly Review of Literature Poetry Series: 50th Anniversary Anthology.*

Cover art by Jill Eggers.

ISBN: 1-878851-06-3

Silverfish Review, P.O. Box 3541, Eugene, OR 97403

CONTENTS

New York Movie, 1939   7

Radiography   9

Incarnations   15
     1. Prelude
     2. Passacaglia
     3. Nocturne
     4. Toccata
     5. Tombeau

Reports   23
     1. Acoustic Shadows
     2. Photograph of the 5th Vermont at Camp Griffin,
       Virginia
     3. Postcard from Cold Harbor
     4. The Confederate Dead
     5. Taps

The Possible   29

for Scott Cairns
Marjorie Maddox

NEW YORK MOVIE, 1939

Homage to Edward Hopper

Under an hourglass of lamplight,
the dim stair shuttles a tireless nothing.
It could be noon for all we know.

The usherette leans, silent, alone,
a deep blue shadow buttoned high
around her pale throat. The ribbon

on her pant leg shines thin as a fuse.
All around her the late are slipping out
of their coats, hushed and believing,

in each eye the glint and the fattening
reel that drives their own black tape.
Here in the dark, they grow defenseless.

The projector beam burns back the layers
of its plot, and they part their lips to watch.
But for her it is the same gray strip

along the optic nerve: a few words broken
in lust and anger, the blurred roulette,
a tumbling car. She stares at carpets,

clicks the flashlight in her hand.
But then what did she expect? Nothing.
Which is to say too much too well: all

in a day's work, she thinks, this idling
on the fringe of worlds too familiar
or strange to respond: this dark,

this room, this great stone column
the color of smoke. Her red rim
of flashlight brushes a man's sleeve.

Then it begins: though just what it is
she cannot say or prefers not to,
not even to herself. It simply comes,

the way squares of sunlight well up
on the side of a house, a corner office,
a quiet meal; or the way a bare white room opens out

onto the sea, how its merely being there
takes a certain freedom of movement.
It's as though solitude were the clear glass

of a painting we love, a cold drink
standing by a window in New England.
It is the lighthouse abandoned to the day,

what frees us to sink obsessed, the way sun sinks
into the eyelids of women on porticos,
what it presses into the warm stone.

Or there, in the red shadow splashed over
the foyer like a gown, the shush of waves
and usherettes so close we too are all

flashlight and stealth. Our very silence
tapers off into something else, more alive,
to part the fiery stillness of her curtain.

RADIOGRAPHY

Nights like this my body would open
the iron door of a deeper rest.
Snow falls in a shower of pins.

It lights up out of nowhere
in the glowing radius of our house.
And all around me, the little clicks

of appliances and hot pipe,
this year's hatch of winter fleas,
the way our room contracts into

the cold hours, the way it swells.
My sleep has never been so sheer.
My husband slips into bed late

and mumbles, pulls the sheet to his lips
with a moan that is part comfort,
part complaint. I think of him

as two people longing to converge.
He cannot resolve the shapes
of questions, disagreements, whatever

leans into the half that listens.
Tempting, to take our wakefulness
with us, to lie face-down

in our wild hair, hands buried,
fingers curved like a watch-
maker god at a small creation.

Not that I am any less
the stranger to my husband's work,
his solitude, but I can't stop seeing

that room, those books, his photos
of the failing lamps in bodies.
There are days they could be anyone's:

this feathery shade of veins,
the pale oval lake of the bladder.
There in its glass, a glint of scars.

Last night by the subway window,
I watched my tired reflection
give way to the emergent light

of Oak Street Station and briefly revived.
As a native I tend to keep
my distance, but there on the live steps

I listened to the tenor player
bite into his reed and solo,
wincing over the high reaches and god

if I didn't envy the body
inside his body. He comes down
most days with an Orphean resolve,

his face afire in its skull-cap,
especially deep into the ends
of phrases. It's as though the harder

he locks into the bright apple
of his sound, the more his breath
leads him, even as he shapes it,

raising up what his hands remember,
his black case gleaming with quarters,
eyes closed. Perfect health, my husband

once said, is a picture of night,
clear and starless, without fate.
What then does a body tell

anyone of the life it leads
into pleasure? Only a nonsense
of aches and wishes, a falling off

into memory and other bodies,
a shade younger perhaps, more faint,
wrapped in the sheer fabric

of our looking on. I never told
my husband how it is sometimes,
how old encounters reemerge less

as a past than the unresolved
shapes of promise after promise.
I never told my husband all

the palmist said of what she saw there
and who, or what she thought I wanted
in her care to leave things open.

In her young hands, my heartline
lay under the stitch of tracks
tunneling into the white ore.

It's something I do for myself,
my husband being further from such things,
skeptical. I like to believe

we agree unscathed in our slight
withholdings, not to mention
the desires we keep from ourselves.

Though they rise beneath my knowing,
trailing in the intricate music,
the idea of them precedes me.

Say you wake up some night stunned
in refrigerator light,
staring into the vestibule,

and realize how little thought
it took to carry you there:
already you grow too large to return.

When the door closes, your shadow
becomes the room you're in.
You walk back to bed, a chill

of milk clinging to your lips.
In my best dream, I am no less
blind: I close my eyes to kiss,

listen, to go forward in my sleep.
Or like Beethoven in his death mask,
to sink into a deep sensation.

I've seen my husband like that:
contemplating a word he's lost,
still groggy under the booth

of rain our bay windows make.
There's scarcely a nerve below
he would not turn down like sheets.

In my favorite *Twilight Zone,*
what I love most is the moment
of discovery, when the boy who gets

his one wish for x-ray vision,
so thrilled to see his girlfriend
whole, burns a channel of sight

past the brief arrival of skin
to the weird labor of her
physical heart. He gazes clear

into its chambers, though only
for a moment there, and through,
where suddenly we find ourselves

at the morning end of a mere dream.
We're a kind of radium that way,
outwardly serene, the bits of us

sparking under our eyelids.
It's how I picture the inventors
of heaven, the way they bow their heads

in a heightening of senses.
They are leaning over something
glittering in the dark, some plate

of water with the sky in it.
Never so clear as in that silence
before a big meal in winter;

just inches from their grateful teeth,
the cooked meat perspiring.
Who can condemn them for the world

they've made, the beautiful machines
of cathedral organs, that wine-
red glass and wax smoke? It sweetens

their bread to think of it: the idea
of a buried, more brilliant life.
They take it on their tongues,

douse the little flames there,
and mumble sleeplessly. To take
and be taken. Not to reject

the world, but to finish it
in their minds, to give it an end
as if it too were a body,

beautiful once and driven,
to hold it the way one body
holds another, how we hold our own,

looking down in bathroom showers
at the slow fuse of being alive.
These nights I lie still as glass

and feel my very cells divide,
alert to sleep or a husband's touch.
Mostly I drift off just this side

of dawn. The snow, if it snows,
turns clear in the black dirt.
Each cold seed is opening.

INCARNATIONS

1. Prelude

Emily winds her metronome
and lets it walk out of her hands.

She slips her fingers into the silent
shape of her first chord—skeptical,

meticulous. By now it's gone
on ahead into the blackened

cadence, through the voluptuous
grief in its path, held notes

decaying under the curved blades of slurs.
She lets herself drag and rush,

swerve over the hills: to drift
is to resist. To surrender both hands,

hurl them as one music at another,
it's how she gives her body

to the difficult, how the difficult
refuses. She rubs her palms,

begins again from the double bar.
The way the metronome moves,

you would think it traveled nothing
but an unbroken, Euclidean line.

She hesitates, listens as it veers
with a slight stagger, nodding

off into silence. Still
she hears it step into the unlit

music in her hands, the spool
of its one eye, uncoiling.

2. Passacaglia

Before wings, before the slightest desire
for wings, she thinks only of the ground
beneath her, there in the organ pedals,

the unsettled terrain she steps softly over,
slow at first, then slower, her feet shy
as giant, misshapen hands, descending

toward some final boredom and release,
when having walked so far into solitude
she feels indistinguishable from the sound

she makes: she could play it in her sleep.
And so the variations as they spring up
through her thighs, her torso, over her shoulders,

the clear veins that wrap around her arms
and perish. She breaks into several bodies
conversing, swept up in the general spirit—

what the arm said, the incredulous ear.
As the bass swells, the basilica shakes,
abandoned, save for the angels forever

surprised through an explosion of ribbons,
clutching their tiny, useless coronets.
All as if they too had losses to bury

in the music, some hand to discipline, a breath.
And what keeps them in their heaven is the same
perishable nakedness she knows

desire by. How bewildered they must be,
to bluster that way into silent horns,
their fingers aching. She feels them haloing

the loft like handsome and predatory birds.
Or falling, as angels will, through the feathered
flames in her hands, her legs. Light as ash.

3. Nocturne

Emily lays the dwindled boat of her hand
on the keys and floats it into a cold blur.
With every dissonance she leaves behind
a watery gash in the strings' black harbor.

In time the very walls go dark: somewhere
other hands are snapping off the light.
It's how they listen best: they disappear
and who can blame them? Who wouldn't lie

vanishing under the blade, this keel
as it carves its fading v in the clear slate?
And for what? as if what lights conceal
were more than sound brimming over the plate

of a piano, resurging into rooms
in waves. She repeats, and the melody curves
like cities, bent along the hazardous rims
of their rivers and parks, the wild preserves.

She loves how the current draws its sure
file of silt, as if her deepest wish
is in this moving on, its coarse erasure,
and the joy that darts inward like a fish.

4. Toccata

Emily closes her eyes and scans
             the Braille of her piano,
        her voice humming darkly in its throat,

her pale hands drawn to the cold
             of each new place, of passing through it
        the way a salamander slips

into ice-green water, shivering
             and precise, the way a drop
        of morphine enters the blood.

With every motion, she sends a chill
             into the black lid and things
        that lie there: the stone head

of a dead composer, an empty glass.
             And outside in the red branches,
        through the veils of flies

in thickets, the stunned world breeding
             its migratory cracks, her music
        blooms like a cloud of dust.

It's what she practices alone
             at night, what the right hand fingers
        on a pillowslip beside her,

as if to find rest in this constant
             moving, the way a tongue moves
        in and out of the words it speaks.

The art is the thing that continually dies
             young and desired, that nearly persuades
        a body of its freedom: its hand

enters the silk lining of her arm
                and glides down to the point of departure.
       Everything she touches now

turns away in bright pieces
              like so many locusts fleeing a fire.
       Whatever price her solitude—

her sore fingers, the green sticks
              burning—that's part of what she craves
       and how she craves it: sleep

or no sleep, it's all she can do
              to begin again like a chain-smoker
       palming a match. And to think

it feels a little like exaltation—
              which it is—like fear's
       white shadow, breath after breath.

5. Tombeau

In the white shadow of a black key,
where the voice you hear is a thin and icy rivulet,

Emily wades just so far
as if time would make a place for her there.

With each dissolution, her palms revive,
empty: a mist of strength emerges through her sleeves.

Isn't it, she thinks, in spite
of the little inflammations

and foretellings, the hidden fumes,
isn't it an embodied need that opens

toward some sinuous devotion in the end?
What else draws a woman so faithfully

down the tenement street from nothingness,
walking for the mere sensation?

There's a morning hunger that presses
her dreaming back into the world.

And what is Emily's piano if not a harp
asleep in its coffin, ghost harp

after harp relinquished from its strings?
It quiets her, to think there are those

who inherit this music, cut and blossoming,
as if the sound's decay is how

they clarify themselves. She rests,
a word poised on the tips of her fingers,

then lays her hands back down on the silence.
The slightest touch and stillness

too has a shape that fails it.
On its skin, the frail thrill, a shudder.

REPORTS

1. Acoustic Shadows

From only a few miles away, a battle sometimes made no sound,
despite the flash and smoke of cannon and the fact that more distant
observers could hear it clearly.

As Lee pushed North and the dead flew
out of the fields in thick flocks
over Pennsylvania, the first, strange reports
went up over the wire:

from the medical tents on Wilson's Hill,
people could see the cannons
driving their nails of light
into the boarded house of the Union

and hear none of it. Who would have
believed things would go this far,
this long, the indestructible world
their intimate stranger?

For the Union soldier bound up
in what he saw, high in the near
silence, history was out there
beating its wings against the glass.

He would not move for the sight of it
and cupped his bowl of boiled coffee, watching.
All night men returned through the wild orchard,
their hands trembling like paper.

The wounded lay out on blankets in rows,
sleepless under the clear sky,
and the nails of remembered light
pinned them to their bodies.

2. Photograph of the 5th Vermont at Camp Griffin, Virginia

They would shake off the blanket of their shapes,
the black blurs that are horses and flags.
They would make a sport of it. A lark.
This much is clear. The avant mare tosses
the smoking cloud of his head unaware
of the photographer's count, the shutter
as it snips its measured ribbon of light.

The closer we look, the stronger the illusion
pulling away, leading us over the Braille
of a day in June, late, each man posed
to advance on the thin board of his shadow.
Here and there the details of lives beckon
with a small white heat: rings, teeth,
the grains of sun clinging to their fingers.

They will remember themselves, cautious
under the spry branches of Virginia.
They will remember themselves. And farther out,
more horses, flags; the river draped
over the earth like a photographer's cloak.

3. Postcard from Cold Harbor

So kind of you to write, to send this autumn
battlefield from Virginia, remembering how
I'm taken by the place: these flames of grass,
that monument sunk in the living embers.
And a sky not heaven but its frightened mirror,
the one bright cloud locked and floating.

I keep thinking of them there, the men
who stitched their names and cities in their shirts,
too serene as they spread their sewing
by the fire, pulled each wet thread between
their lips and slipped it into the needle's eye.

They narrowed their vision to see it,
making themselves small, sharp: so in time
they might follow the path of their letters,
so they might be carried off still warm
and shouldered into granary carts,
divided each from each. Under the idle
flapping of the coroner's tent, their names
would float from the patches on their backs,
sent out for a sheet of marble to lie in.

There would be voices to pronounce them,
the more difficult sounds repeated as questions.
And for a while it would seem generous
to talk this way, as if the names were so
many cases to tend to, for a year
or two, a generation at very most.
It would seem a kind of personal reply:
the quiet surrounding these words like parks.

4. Confederate Dead

Small comfort, to have survived your name
and body, given over to the false tints
of painted slides, though, as we are often
led to believe, a dead man could do worse,

as in one of those accidents of charity
when the images were sold cheap, for the glass
at the heart of their tragic sentiment,
thousands of photographic slides raised
into the roofs of greenhouses. Go there.

See for yourself. Impossible as it is
to make out the red translucent cloth
and fire, the fog of sleeves, to trace
the man where he stood among so many

past misfortune he must have seemed
a phantom to himself. You never know.
You too might look up some day at the sheer
sky through the center of his body.

It takes a forgetful mind to enter the past
completely, the way we eventually do,
in our dotage perhaps or still later.
Or like the invisible man shell-
shocked from all feeling in his arm.

This too is how to survive your life,
to draw blanks over an effulgence
of scallions, blood tomatoes, the thick green air,
to be made singular in a true sense.

Or if not to survive it, to consume it
the way fire consumes itself, concealing.
Denial is like that, however ceremonious
or slight. The past eats and is eaten,

though it sometimes helps to think of this
as mercy. And it is. It takes years
of sun to bleach a phantom arm or flag, to turn
the way a widow turns her grief to her child.

No telling who she looks through now.
It's a comfort to think the dead there,
though they were always closest as a hunger,
a sinking into warm glass, unshattered, clear.

5. Taps

As night fell and the end of the world
brushed Atlanta with its black wing

beating a path through the embers,
men on either hill lowered their work

and looked up, listening. Somewhere
a rebel trumpet played slow and clear:

straight tones rustling vaguely at the ends.

Trees filled out their thin shirts.
The newly dead bent down in long arcs

into the circled breath of the boy.
There pressed against his teeth,

the force of grace reddened his tongue,
his cheeks, sweetened on his lips.

For a time the world burned unattended.
The sky's door swung gently on its hinge.

Music rolled in the beds of stones, grass,
all things and the breath that held their fire.

THE POSSIBLE

Once they were all we knew in the world,
the shapes of prayers and questions rising;
in radiant cribs, they curved up at the ends
of our voices. There was much to believe.
By a potted palm in the broken sun,

we felt them on our tongues like milk.
They slipped out of the names we gave them.
Once they rose in the wells of our bodies,
sprouted as hairs where the soil was darkest.
It was all we could do to keep them down.

Nights they backed away into the future
gazing at the body of the past, spread
themselves like a bride before a mirror.
We stood up too charmed to sleep and listened.
They made light of threats, promises.

When we cut them in two, each half-shuddered
in a fierce dream, they gave praise to no end.
How we wanted it to go on that way,
the evenings we stripped like oranges,
the soft, declarative fist of the heart.

But already we owed our lives to days
that refuse to straighten but come back
drifting in their arc, broken by horizons,
bearing down where we bend to drink, mourn,
brace ourselves for the world's return.

Bruce Bond's collections of poetry include *The Ivory Hours* (Heatherstone Press), *Independence Days* (Robert Gross Award, Woodley Press), *The Anteroom of Paradise* (Colladay Award, Quarterly Review of Literature), and *Broken Circle* (Ring of Fire Award, Archangel Books). Presently he is an Assistant Professor of Creative Writing at Wichita State University.